ater
CIELO

Rachel Katstaller

Orchard Books
Scholastic Inc.
New York

Cielo loved to skateboard.
She had a steezy push and a good pop,
and sometimes it looked like she was flying.

When she had a board under her feet,
her ordinary town transformed . . .

into the most extraordinary skate park.

Sidewalks became obstacles to ollie up,

rails turned into hippie jumps,

and streets changed into speedy downhill rides.

When she skated, nothing could stop her.

One day, a park with deep pools opened.
The biggest pool looked high from the top —
super high.

And from the bottom it looked
like the mouth of a whale,
so that's what everyone called it.

All the skaters were crazy about it,
and Cielo was, too.

Cielo waited for her turn at The Whale.
Then, as she had seen the others do, she dropped in.

She fumbled . . .

and tumbled . . .

and slammed to a stop next to her board.

She got up on shaky legs.
She wasn't hurt, but she'd never fallen like that before.

SKATE RAMS
SKATE RAMS

Cielo hurried out of the skate park.
If she couldn't skate The Whale,

at least she could still do her ollies,

land hippie jumps,

and ride downhill . . .

Cielo couldn't stand it.
She lost her cool.

Cielo walked home and shoved her skateboard into the back of her closet.

She didn't want to look at it ever again.

INDÉPENDE
ESKEIT
SKA
RA
the
SKATE RATS
vol.7

Whenever Cielo passed the skate park, she'd see The Whale from a distance and shiver.

"Hey!" a girl shouted.
"Didn't you use to skate?"
"I'm the worst skateboarder in the world,"
Cielo mumbled.
"No, you're not! I've seen what you can do.
Come and skate with me and Miro!"

Cielo's new friends, Mia and Miro, were great skaters.
Together, they zoomed in and out of the pool.
Sometimes it looked like they were flying.
Cielo watched them in awe.
She wanted to fly again, too,
but all she could think about was falling.

With her helmet secured, her knee pads and elbow pads on, Cielo looked over the edge into the mouth of The Whale.

It was a big drop. Bigger than she remembered.
"Go, Cielo!" Miro cheered.
"You can do this!" Mia shouted.
"I can do this," she told herself.

She ignored her shaky knees.
And dropped in.

She flew, then tumbled, and slammed so hard
that tears were forced out of her eyes.
"I can't do this!" Cielo cried.

Miro skated up. "What do you mean? You just did!"
"But I slammed!" said Cielo.
"Yeah, and it was super sick!" said Mia.

Cielo blinked and sat up. Her stomach did a flip, but it wasn't the falling kind.
She was suddenly feeling a little more fierce.

Cielo climbed out of The Whale
and looked over the edge.
Her brain felt foggy with fear,
but her friends' cheers rang out loud and clear.

"One more time!"
"You've almost got it!"
"Just lean into it — it feels like flying!"
There was nothing that Cielo
loved more than flying.
So she dropped in again . . .

. . . and again,

and again,

and again . . .

SKATE
RATAS

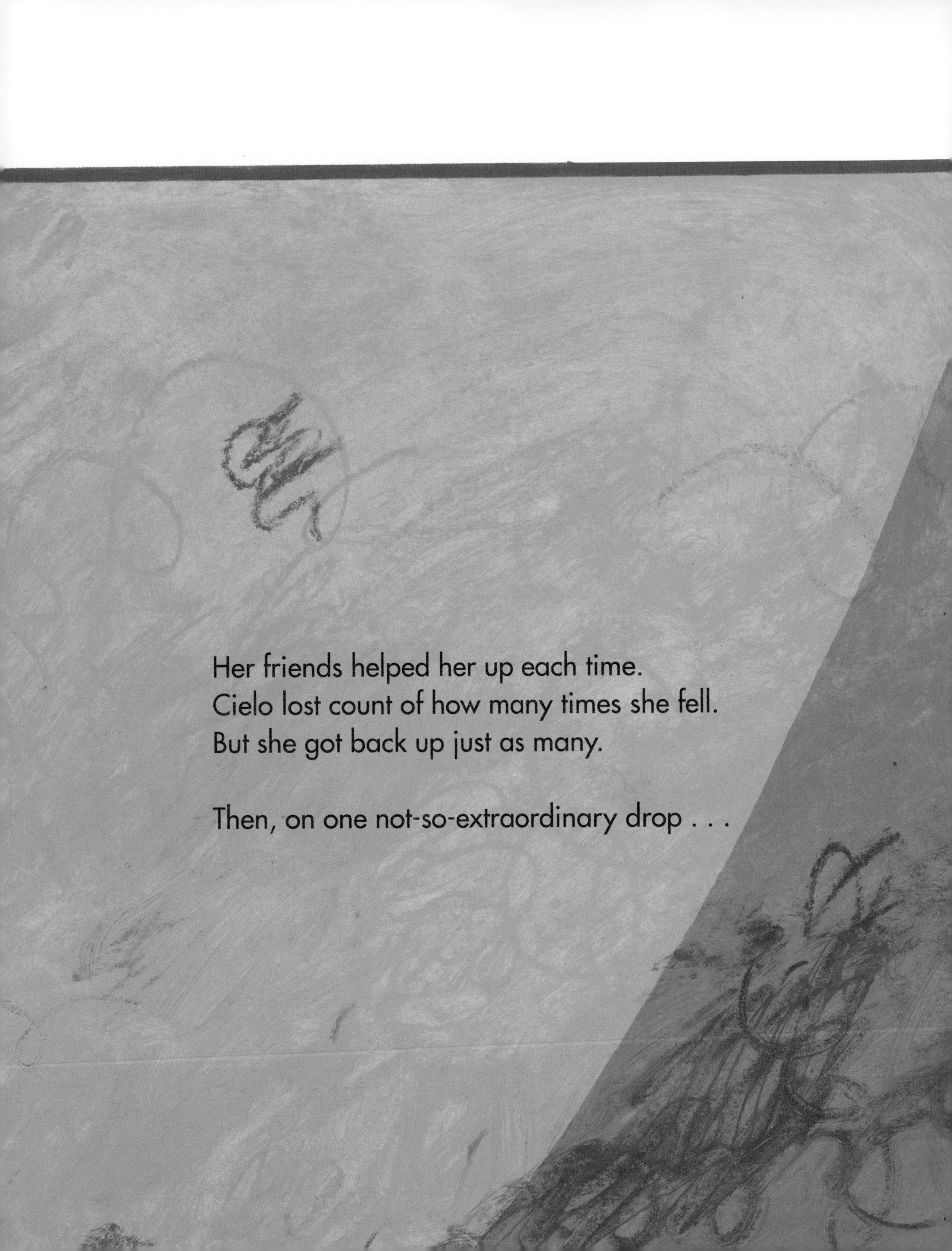

Her friends helped her up each time.
Cielo lost count of how many times she fell.
But she got back up just as many.

Then, on one not-so-extraordinary drop . . .

Cielo flew as high as she had ever flown.

GLOSSARY

steezy: stylish

steezy push: a way to describe a skater's stylish way of moving forward with a skateboard

pop: how high a skater can jump by striking the tail of the board against the ground

hippie jump: when the board slides under a rail/obstacle while the skater jumps above it and lands on top of the board again after clearing the obstacle

ollie: the most important skateboarding trick; involves jumping by popping the tail of the board on the ground and lifting it (depicted below)

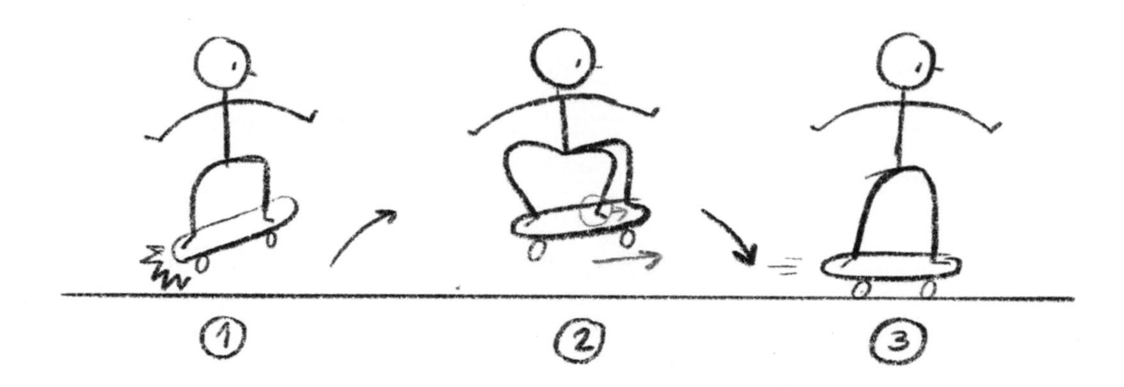

drop in: when a skater tips down into a ramp or steep transition

transition: the curvature of a skate ramp, pool, bowl, and mini-ramp

pool: concrete ramps in the shape of a swimming pool that (in its inception used to) imitate waves

vert: The Whale is a vert ramp, a half pipe (or big transition) with a beginning section of 2–3 feet that is completely vertical

AUTHOR'S NOTE

Skateboarding is not only a sport, and most recently an Olympic sport, but also mainly a community of like-minded people. This book is a small celebration of this community that has welcomed me with open arms ever since I began skateboarding not too long ago. I have had the opportunity to meet and skate with people from all over the world, in so many different countries, and it's always been a profound joy to share the passion and creativity behind skateboarding.

And just as I have been encouraged by strangers, who have become my dearest skater girlfriends, I hope this book encourages others to experience friendships and community, to get up after failing again and again, to finally land that trick after hours of trying, and most importantly, to feel the sheer joy of pushing those four wheels on concrete.